When Grandma and Grandpa visited Alaska they ...

To Garrett & Hannah
Enjoy this tour through beautiful
Alaska!

... came to see the many wonderful things
this state has to offer. They were very excited
to finally see Alaska for themselves,
after they had read and heard so much about
its beautiful scenery and wild animals.
This is the story of their adventurous journey.

Denali Park, Alaska, July 1, 2003

Acknowledgements:
We are grateful to Bob and Pam Gilbertson for their support during this book project; to my brother, Ingo Richter, for his technical help in Germany; to editing consultant Lynne Beykirch for her review and suggestions; to Regina Neely, Pam "The Grammar Cop" Patterson, and our "Saddle Pals" Kasey Goss and Scott Danforth for their constructive criticism and words of encouragement; to Jim Miller for hardware support; and to Cindy and Wray Kinard for providing hugs when needed the most.

> To our parents and grandparents, who never had the opportunity to visit this great land.

Other children's books by Bernd and Susan Richter available through Saddle Pal Creations, Inc.:

* When Grandma Visited Alaska She ...
* Grandma and Grandpa Love Their RV
* Uncover Alaska's Wonders (a lift-the-flap book)
* How Alaska Got Its Flag
* Do Alaskans Live in Igloos?
* Alaska Animals - Where Do They Go at 40 Below?
* Come Along and Ride the Alaska Train
* The Twelve Days of Christmas in Alaska
* The Little Bear Who Didn't Want to Hibernate
* Cruising Alaska's Inside Passage
* All Aboard the White Pass & Yukon Route Railroad
* Goodnight Alaska - Goodnight Little Bear (board book)
* Peek-A-Boo Alaska (lift-the-flap board book)
* How Animal Moms Love Their Babies (board book)

www.alaskachildrensbooks.com

When Grandma and Grandpa visited Alaska they ...

A Children's Book
by
Bernd and Susan Richter

Published by
Saddle Pal Creations, Cantwell, Alaska

Do you know where Alaska is? If you were in a space-ship high above the earth and if you then looked out the window, this is what you would see. Where you live is probably somewhere in the red or tan areas. Can you find your home on this map? If you can't, Grandma or Grandpa will help you. They will also show you where they and some of your other relatives live. If you live in the lower 48 states, to get to Alaska (shown in dark blue) from where you live, you have to travel through an entire other country, called Canada. If you live in Canada, maybe you have to travel as far or further than some of the American kids. Can you see why? If your home isn't on this map, then you live very, very far away. If Alaska is so far away, how do you think Grandma and Grandpa got there?

The fastest way for Grandma and Grandpa to get to Alaska probably would be by airplane. Can you guess how long such a flight would take from where you live? Ask Grandma or Grandpa if that is how they got to Alaska, how long the flight took, and if they enjoyed the flight. Have you ever flown? If so, did you like it? If you haven't been in an airplane yet, would you like to one day?

In Alaska, there are two major cities, Anchorage and Fairbanks. Ask Grandma or Grandpa to show you where those cities are on the map on the cover of this book. Most of the big airplanes land in these cities. Grandma or Grandpa will tell you if they visited these cities and what they did there.

If Grandma and Grandpa didn't get to Alaska by airplane, they may have traveled by ship. Every summer, cruise ships sail north to bring visitors to this faraway land. Do you know what a cruise ship is or have you perhaps seen one? They are huge ships. Cruise ships have space for hundreds of passengers. Because those ships are on the ocean for many days at a time, they have bedrooms for all the passengers and crew. They also have dining rooms and shops. The biggest cruise ships even have swimming pools! Some people like to take their cars with them on the ship to Alaska. Those ships are called ferries. Ask your Grandma or Grandpa if they took a ship to Alaska and what kind it was. If they didn't take a ship this time, ask them if they ever have been on one. And how about you? Have you been on a ship? Tell Grandma or Grandpa about your boating adventures.

INSIDE PASSAGE

From the ship, passengers see the coast and the big mountains of Alaska. Some of these mountains are so high that the snow on them never melts. As the snow gets thicker with each winter, glaciers are formed. A glacier is like a river made of snow and ice. Over time, it gets so heavy that it starts to slowly move down from the high mountains to the low coast. It's just like a snowball rolling downhill, only much slower. At the coast, the ice breaks off into the water. It is then called an iceberg. Ask Grandma or Grandpa if they saw any glaciers or icebergs. What do you think happens to icebergs? Will they float or will they sink to the bottom of the ocean? Find out when you take your next bath. Ask your mom or dad to put some ice cubes into your bath water. Then watch what happens to the ice.

People on the ships enjoy watching the animals that live in the ocean. Can you name any animals that live in the water? Have you ever heard of a sea otter? In Alaska, everybody likes to watch sea otter families, because they are so cute and playful, just like children. They often swim right next to the ships, eating crabs and clams. They do that while floating on their backs, which is very easy for them because they have a thick fur coat that works like an air mattress. Grandma or Grandpa will tell you if and where they saw any of those cute sea otters.

Do you know who Willy the Whale is? In the waters off the coast of Alaska, there still live many friends of Willy. The whales can be seen when they occasionally come to the surface. Then the tops of their heads are visible during breathing, and the tails are visible before they dive under the water. But when they're playing and when they're having lots of fun, they sometimes even jump out of the water, just like Willy did when he escaped to be free. Ask Grandma or Grandpa if they saw a whale in Alaska and how big it was. Did you know that some whales can be as long as a huge truck with a trailer?

Many birds live along the coast. Some of those are the same kinds of birds as you might find in your backyard. Others only live in faraway places, such as Alaska. One of these is the puffin, shown in this picture. With its yellow and red beak and with its orange legs and feet, it can be seen from far away. Have you ever seen such a funny-looking bird? Are there any similar funny-looking birds where you live? Can you name any birds that live in your backyard?

The ships stop at cities and towns along the coast where the passengers can get off for some sightseeing. Then some people go shopping while others go to see the totem poles, which often decorate houses and parks in certain areas of Alaska. Do you know what a totem pole is? Totem poles are carved by native people of Alaska out of very tall trees. The carvings show faces of people and different animals, such as frogs, birds, and fish. These faces and animals tell family stories, just like a picture book tells a story. Can you find any frogs on these totem poles? What else can you find?

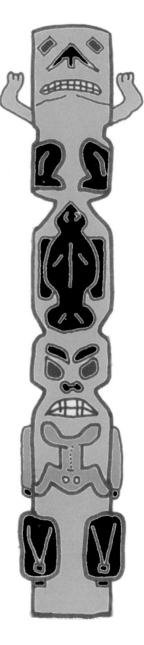

Since Alaska is a very big state, many visitors take
a train to see more of the land. The train runs from
the coast to the city of Fairbanks in the middle of
the state. On the way, passengers can see huge
mountain ranges, including Mt. McKinley, North
America's highest mountain, large forests, big rivers,
and sometimes even wild animals. Have you ever
been on a train? If not, would you like to ride on
one? Maybe Grandma and Grandpa will take you
on a train   trip someday.

The train in Alaska stops at Denali National Park, where many wild animals live. This park is like a very, very big zoo but without any fences. All the animals, even the big grizzly bears, can wander around wherever they want looking for something to eat and for a place to sleep. They have to look for their own food, because people are not allowed to feed the animals like you can in a zoo. The animals are wild here and should be kept wild so that they can take care of themselves when there are no people around. In this picture, can you find some of the animals that live in the park? Can you show Grandma or Grandpa the bear, the wolf, the caribou, and the moose? Ask Grandma or Grandpa what animals they saw when they visited Denali.

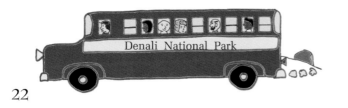

Did you find the moose? If not, here is a bigger one for you to see. Moose are usually even bigger than horses. Do they live near you, too? They can be recognized easily by their big antlers, which grow on their heads each year. Can you think of any other animals that have antlers? Or how about animals with horns? Can you think of animals with horns? Do any of those live in your area? If so, tell Grandma or Grandpa about them.

Do you know what kind of food moose like? Often you can see them feeding in small lakes. Could they be eating fish? No, they don't eat fish! They eat the green grasses that grow on the bottom of lakes, but their favorite food is leaves from alder bushes. They also like to hide in the bushes during the day.

Have you ever seen a bear -- not a teddy bear but a real bear? One place to see bears would be in a zoo. They are kept in cages or behind big walls in zoos because bears can be very dangerous. In Alaska, bears still live in the wild. In the spring you can see them with their babies, which were born during the last winter and now like to play in the meadows after all the snow is gone. Mama bear watches so that nobody comes too close to her babies. That is why Grandma and Grandpa had to stay far away and hide when they watched the bears. Do you think Grandma and Grandpa were scared when they saw the bears in the wild? Would you have been scared?

Where the trains can't go, Grandma and Grandpa may have traveled by car. Maybe they even drove all the way to Alaska. A lot of people get off the airplanes or ships and rent vehicles. This could be a camper vehicle a lot like the one in this picture. Those are great for travel because they have a kitchen, a bed, and a bathroom right inside. This way, Grandma and Grandpa could have camped wherever they wanted. Have you ever seen or been in a camper? Do you think you would like to sleep in a camper or in a tent? When it rains, would you rather be in a camper or in a tent? Which is better on a mountain top, the tent or the camper? Ask Grandma or Grandpa if they tried camping while they were in Alaska.

Many people come to Alaska because there are still many big fish in the rivers. Every summer, hundreds of thousands of fish called salmon swim from the ocean up the rivers to the places where they were born a few years earlier. People go to the rivers to either watch them or to catch the fish. Ask Grandma or Grandpa if they saw some red salmon and if they possibly even caught some. Do you eat fish? These fish taste very good!

Some people don't go to the rivers for the fish. Instead, they may go there to search for gold, which can be found in the ground along some of the rivers in Alaska. Do you know what gold is? If so, can you name or show Grandma or Grandpa something that is made from gold? If not, maybe they can help you. To find gold, a miner puts rocks and dirt into a pan and then washes it in river water. This is hard work because a lot of rocks and dirt have to be carried to the river and washed and because the river water is very cold. If the miner is lucky, like the one in this picture, there will be gold left in the pan after all the rocks and dirt are washed away. A few people have become very rich doing this, but most find little or no gold for their hard work.

Because Alaska is located far to the
north, a strange thing happens
during the summer months.

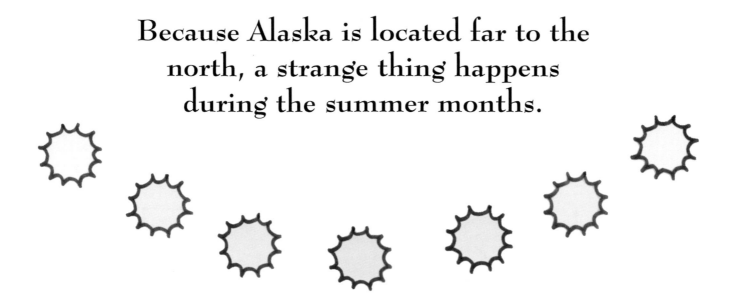

Can you imagine a place where it doesn't get dark at
night? Alaska is like that during the summer. It
doesn't get dark because just when the sun is about
to set for the evening, it rises again to begin the next
day. Then, people and animals go to bed very, very
late, and children can still play outside in daylight
when it is dark already where you live. Would you
like that? Do you think you could sleep at all if it
didn't get dark at night?

34

In winter,
just the opposite
happens with the sun.
On some days, the sun
never comes up in the morning,
and it remains dark throughout
the day. This is a good time to see the
northern lights in the dark skies. Northern lights
are bands of gray, green, and pink colors that swirl
around as if someone had turned on a huge multi-colored flashlight and pointed it at the sky. When
that happens, people like to go outside to watch
them, just like people watch fireworks on the 4th
of July. Ask Grandma or Grandpa if they have seen
the northern lights. Ask them, too, if you can see
them in the winter where you live.

In the northernmost part of Alaska by the North Pole, where it is so cold that the entire ocean is filled with ice and icebergs, lives Alaska's largest land animal, the polar bear. Because not many animals live in the frozen North, polar bears have to be good hunters to find their food. What helps them to be good hunters is their white fur coat, which makes them difficult to see on the snow-covered ice. This also makes them very dangerous for people, because the polar bear thinks people are food. Not many people go to see polar bears in the wild. Instead, they go to a zoo to see polar bears. Have you been to a zoo? Did you see a bear there? If you haven't, maybe Grandma and Grandpa will take you one day to see one.

At a time almost as long ago as
when the dinosaurs lived, an
animal even bigger than the polar
bear -- the woolly mammoth --

made its home in Alaska. The woolly mammoth looked
a lot like an elephant, but it had very long fur. You've
seen an elephant, haven't you? Today, there are no
mammoths left in Alaska, so Grandma and Grandpa
couldn't have seen them in the wild. But maybe one of
your ancient relatives saw them a long time ago while
in Alaska. Can you find the people who might be those
old relatives in the picture?
Once in a while, the bones of mammoths are found by
people digging holes. These bones are then brought to
museums for display. Ask Grandma or Grandpa to take
you to such a museum one day. There are usually a lot
of neat things to do and see in a museum.

After Grandma and Grandpa visited all these great places and saw all these wild animals and other interesting things, it was time for them to go home again. They were really looking forward to again seeing their family, their friends and neighbors, and especially you! Because they love you, and because they liked Alaska so much, they brought you this pretty picture book as a gift. A few years from now, when you are grown, maybe you will visit Alaska yourself. Maybe then you will remember all the pictures Grandma and Grandpa showed you and all the stories they told you.

Good-bye, Alaska!

Your Travel Log Here

_____

_____

_____

_____

_____

_____

_____

_____

_____

_____

_____

Your Photos Here

Your Travel Log Here

Your Photos Here

Your Travel Log Here